Let's Read!

📖 Read the Page

▶ Read the Story

★ Game

😃 Yes   ☹ No

↻ Repeat

■ Stop

The New Girl!

Doc McStuffins has a secret. When she puts on her stethoscope, it *sparkles,* and her stuffed animals and toys come to life!

Doc fixes her toys when they have problems. She hopes to be a doctor like her mom when she grows up, because then she can fix people, too.

One day, Doc received a surprise in the mail. Her grandma had sent her a toy from **Japan!** Doc took the new toy to her clinic.

She put on her stethoscope, and the toys crowded around.

"Who's the new girl?"
asked Hallie the hippo.

"I'm Kiko!" came a muffled voice from inside the package. She'd been standing in the box for a very long time. Doc released the ties so Kiko could move her arms and legs.

"Arigatō gozaimasu!" Kiko said.

"That's 'thank you' in Japanese."

"Why do you speak Japanese?" asked Lambie.

"Because I'm from Japan," said Kiko.

Doc pointed to Japan on the globe.

7

"I'm an action toy!"

Kiko said. "Check out my big move!"

She jumped ...

8

... **and fell.** The toys were concerned.

"Whoa! That was weird," said Kiko.

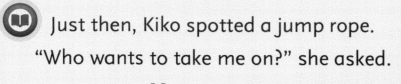

Just then, Kiko spotted a jump rope. "Who wants to take me on?" she asked.

Hallie did!

"Hoppin' hippo!"
Hallie chanted as she jumped.

"Nice jumping, Hallie,"
said Doc.

"You're pretty good," said Kiko.
"I have a few moves myself. **Step aside!**"

But, when Kiko tried to jump,
her knees shook.

She fell down.
"There's something wrong
with my legs! They went all
kazooie!" said a worried Kiko.

"I can fix you up," said Doc.

"Time for a checkup!"

Doc showed Kiko a reflex hammer.

"Reflexes are how your muscles move when they're working right," said Lambie.

Doc gently tapped the hammer to Kiko's knee, but it didn't move.

"I have a diagnosis," said Doc.

"This looks like a case of Weak-Muscle-itis."

Doc sketched the diagnosis into

The Big Book of Boo-Boos.

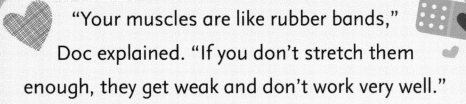

"Your muscles are like rubber bands," Doc explained. "If you don't stretch them enough, they get weak and don't work very well."

Kiko had been in that box all the way from Japan, so her muscles were stiff.

"Can you fix her?" asked Lambie.

"Absolutely," said Doc.

"Tell me what to do!" said Kiko.

"To get your muscles working again, you
need to **stretch and flex!**"
said Doc, showing her how.
Kiko stretched and flexed.

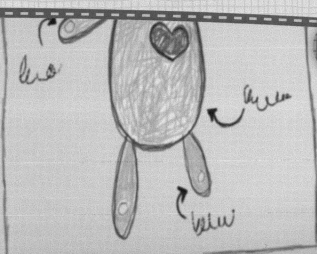

"Look at me! **I'm ready for action**," said Kiko, and she performed her big move perfectly.

"Leaping locusts," declared
Hallie. "She's as limber as a
leopard in a leotard!"

The stretching really helped Kiko.

"Looks like you've saved another toy, Doc," said Lambie. "Nice work."

"Arigatō gozaimasu!" said Doc. "Thanks, Lambie."

Brrrrritis

Pricklethorn

No-Vroom-Vroom-atosis

Un-Bur-Able-Burs

The Dusty-Musties

Driedout-atosis

Mystery Pox

Stinkysalamibreath